15 KB

J
398
Mo

The Adventures of Tom Thumb

Written by
MARIANNA MAYER

Illustrated by
KINUKO Y. CRAFT

SeaStar Books

NEW YORK

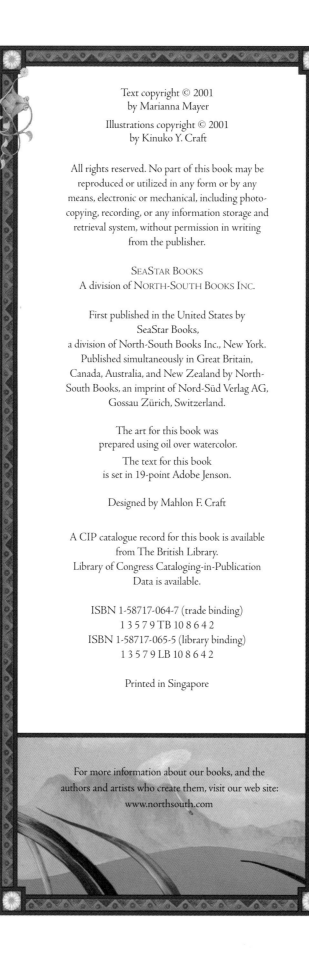

Text copyright © 2001
by Marianna Mayer

Illustrations copyright © 2001
by Kinuko Y. Craft

SEASTAR BOOKS
A division of NORTH-SOUTH BOOKS INC.

First published in the United States by
SeaStar Books,
a division of North-South Books Inc., New York.
Published simultaneously in Great Britain,
Canada, Australia, and New Zealand by North-
South Books, an imprint of Nord-Süd Verlag AG,
Gossau Zürich, Switzerland.

The art for this book was
prepared using oil over watercolor.
The text for this book
is set in 19-point Adobe Jenson.

Designed by Mahlon F. Craft

A CIP catalogue record for this book is available
from The British Library.
Library of Congress Cataloging-in-Publication
Data is available.

ISBN 1-58717-064-7 (trade binding)
1 3 5 7 9 TB 10 8 6 4 2
ISBN 1-58717-065-5 (library binding)
1 3 5 7 9 LB 10 8 6 4 2

Printed in Singapore

For more information about our books, and the
authors and artists who create them, visit our web site:
www.northsouth.com

For Ralph Howard...
a heart as immense as a giant...
a spirit as indomitable as Tom Thumb

M. M.

For all Little People with Big Dreams

uring the reign of King Arthur, wishing made a difference. In that time, which was a very long time ago, kindness was said to bring reward, while the vain and the cruel got their comeuppance in a speedy manner. It was, to be sure, a perfect time for Tom Thumb to be born.

Tall Tim of the Mountains, a farmer by trade, was wed to a good woman named Kate. Together, the old couple shared a single wish to have a child. Nevertheless, they had not one.

ne day, when discussing this, their fondest wish, Tall Tim said to his wife, "I'd gladly forfeit much that is good in our lives if we could have a wee babe of our own. Truly, even if that child were no bigger than my thumb, I should be the happiest man in the land."

Kate thought for a while before answering and then she said, "There is only one thing to do. You must see King Arthur's great wizard, Merlin. With Merlin's knowledge of all that is known and all that is unknown, he'll be the one to help us."

arly one spring morning, Tall Tim set out in search of the wizard. In late afternoon, when the sky was turning soft shades of crimson, he spied an old man. Half hidden in the forest shadows, the white-bearded man was mumbling spells while he bent over to scratch strange marks upon the ground with a long ebony stick.

Just then, the old man looked up and said, "Ah! So it's Tall Tim of the Mountains, at last."

Before Tim could reply, Merlin—for of course that's who the old gentleman was—stepped into a hollow oak tree where he made his home and sat down. "Come in, there's plenty of room, my good fellow. Don't be alarmed, I know why you're here. But it's taken you a long time to decide to see me about it."

And so Tim managed to tell Merlin what was in his heart, concluding with what he had told Kate: "Even if the child were no bigger than my thumb"—he paused to hold up his thumb for emphasis—"I should be the happiest man alive!"

"Is that so?" said Merlin, smiling. "What an interesting idea. Very well then. Go along home; this wish of yours shall be fulfilled."

As Merlin watched Tall Tim set off for home, he whispered these words:

THE MOON
SHALL WAX AND WANE
THREE TIMES BEFORE A CHILD,
BOLDER THAN A GIANT
AND BRAVER THAN A LION,
SHALL BE BORN.
AND THOUGH HE BE NO BIGGER
THAN HIS FATHER'S THUMB,
UNTIL THE WORLD
DOES ENDING COME,
THERE WILL BE STORIES OF
TOM THUMB.

No sooner did three months pass than, as Merlin predicted, a baby was born, but the child was no bigger than his father's thumb and no bigger would he ever grow. It made not a whit of difference to Kate and Tim, however. They were as happy and proud as any two parents could be.

The Queen of the Little People came out from the mist of Fairyland with goblins and elves, sprites and dryads in attendance to see the newborn child. As the Queen gazed upon the tiny boy, she promised to be his fairy godmother and to always watch over him.

"I shall name you Tom Thumb," declared the Queen, "who shall never seem older or younger, bigger or smaller, stronger or weaker than at this moment." At the instant these words were spoken, Tom Thumb reached his full maturity.

From high and low the little people came with gifts for Tom. There was a bright russet oak-leaf made into a hat and trousers of the softest thistledown, shirts and stockings spun by spiders, and a fine pair of snake-skin boots. Last, but surely not least, his fairy god-mother gave him a magical sword.

"If you use it for good," she told him, "this sword will serve you well."

Now on the other side of the kingdom, around the same time, a giant that some called Gembo moved into a deserted castle. Although Kate and Tim were far too delighted with their young son to take much notice, Gembo began to terrorize the countryside. King Arthur called out his knights, but all the King's men could not put an end to the trouble the giant was causing.

Meanwhile Tom Thumb was busy making himself useful to his parents. Dressed in his finery with his sword at his side, he was eager to prove that he could do anything a full-size boy might do, only better—and, as far as Tom Thumb was concerned, that certainly included looking for all kinds of adventure.

One day when Tall Tim was getting his horse harnessed to go ploughing in the field, Tom came running after him and asked to be taken along. His father was worried that Tom might get lost or hurt, but he didn't want to discourage his son.

"Put me into the horse's ear, Father," said Tom Thumb. "You'll see that I can help with the chores."

Tall Tim obliged and off they went across the countryside. The plough horse knew exactly what Tom whispered in her ear, for his fairy godmother had given him the knowledge of how to speak to animals.

"What a wonderful son we have," said Tall Tim to his wife when he and Tom came through the door that evening. "I have never seen man nor boy handle a horse half so well as our Tom Thumb."

om also wanted to help his mother with her work, but here he did not fare quite so well.  At milking time, he sat upon a mound of sweet hay and fed the black-and-white cow. But the cow swallowed Tom along with the hay!

"Oh!" shouted Tom Thumb in the darkness of the cow's throat. "There are no windows or doors in here. How will I get out?" But there was no one to hear while he was inside the cow; even the cow couldn't hear him. What was worse, more and more hay was coming down on top of him. If he didn't think of some-thing soon, he would be on his way to the cow's stomach.

Just then Tom clutched at some hay and began to tickle the cow. The tickling made the cow feel quite odd. She laughed, coughed, sneezed, and laughed again. Suddenly out came Tom. He went flying through the air and landed in a mud puddle.

The puddle seemed as large as a lake to Tom Thumb, but he managed to swim quite well—until a raven, thinking Tom was a curious-looking frog, swooped down in a flash and carried him away.

et me go!" demanded Tom Thumb.

When the raven heard what he thought was a frog speak in his own language, he was so startled that he dropped Tom. Down, down, down Tom fell. He didn't stop falling till he tumbled down a cavernous chimney. At last, he landed at the very bottom of an open hearth.

Tom Thumb had arrived in a splendid castle, but it was occupied by none other than the giant Gembo. The sharp-eyed Gembo looked up from his supper and spied Tom there among the cold ashes. Thinking he was a sprite come to do some mischief, Gembo rushed at him.

But Tom Thumb was too nimble to be caught so easily. No sooner did Gembo reach to grab him than Tom slipped through the giant's huge fingers. Having no place in particular to escape to, Tom ran as fast as he could up the giant's arm and around his elbow and down his back. Just then he saw a mousehole; Tom jumped and was safely inside.

Knocking over tables, chairs, and crockery, Gembo searched for Tom, but he had not seen where the little fellow had gone. In the end, Gembo was in a fury. He grumbled and he roared, but he could not find Tom Thumb that night.

The giant went to bed, but all night long he tossed and turned. He could not sleep for thinking that at any moment the mischievous sprite would creep into his room and do him harm.

t the first light of day, Gembo came into the great hall, bellowing, "Fi, fee, fan, I smell that little mite. But never you mind, Gembo will grind his bones between his teeth tonight!"

This horrid speech terrified poor Tom, who was still hiding in the mousehole. "What shall I do?" wondered Tom. Clearly, there was nowhere to run. He must face the giant or remain in the mousehole for no telling how much longer. Gathering his courage, Tom stepped out into the open.

Gembo was flabbergasted to see such boldness in one so very small. "What do you want here, you dreadful little mite?" asked the giant in a thundering voice.

"I have come to offer my services," announced Tom Thumb. "In return, I ask only food and lodging."

Surprisingly, Gembo accepted the offer. That very day Tom was employed as his little man in charge of the household chores. Indeed, Gembo had to admit that Tom Thumb was quite useful, for no one could chase mice and rats away better. Or sweep cobwebs from corners, or open a lock when the key could not be found. However, Gembo still held a grudge against him, and Gembo never forgot that once he wanted to grind Tom's bones.

ne night, the giant had some meat to roast, and he ordered Tom to cook it. Placing himself before the fire, Tom sat on a wood chip and turned the spit. But the fire was so hot that he held a spoon with his other hand to shield himself from the heat. Seeing Tom so completely engaged gave Gembo an irresistible idea.

hen and there, his evil nature overcame him and he seized Tom. Tossing him into his mouth, the giant decided to grind the little fellow between his teeth without delay. But Tom fled from the giant's teeth and tumbled down into Gembo's stomach, whereupon he kicked up such an awful rumpus that Gembo howled with pain. The giant rolled on his back and he rolled on his belly, he kicked his legs and he howled anew, but the pain was too much for him. At last, he was forced to hang his head over the castle wall and cough and cough, until he coughed up Tom Thumb.

The giant's stomach may have felt better, but his pride was severely wounded. The very idea that he, the fiercest giant in the land, should be outsmarted by a mere mite no bigger than a man's thumb was terribly humiliating. Soon everyone would be laughing at him. Gembo knew what he must do. That very day, he packed his bags and left the countryside, never to bother anyone again.

Meanwhile, Tom Thumb's adventures were not over. After being expelled from the giant's stomach, he plunged into the castle moat, where he was promptly snapped up by an enormous salmon.

Next day, a fisherman caught the fish and brought the handsome prize to King Arthur. Imagine the royal cook's surprise when she opened the fish's stomach and discovered Tom Thumb!

veryone in the castle wanted to see Tom, for he was quite alive and eager to tell his tale to all. When King Arthur learned that Tom Thumb had dispatched the evil giant, he ordered Tom to be brought before him.

"For ridding our kingdom of the terrible giant Gembo, that even the bravest of my company could not defeat, I hereby knight you Sir Tom Thumb—evermore the smallest and the boldest of the crown's protectors."

The King gave Tom a shield all painted with red roses and a fine black mouse to ride when the King's knights went a-hunting. But though he was the darling of the court, soon Tom began to miss his parents. Finally he asked King Arthur if he might go to visit them.

s a parting gift, the King gave him seven white mice to draw his tiny coach and a bag of gold coins with his compliments.

Tom Thumb arrived home to a great and wonderful celebration. Kate and Tim were there to welcome him, and all the little people came out of their hiding places to join in. The festivities went on and on for days and days, and if they haven't grown tired of all their merry-making, it goes on still.

In England in 1791, it was observed that "every city, town, village, shop, stall, man, woman, and child in the kingdom can bear witness" to the popularity of Tom Thumb's story. The earliest surviving text is believed to have been printed in 1621, and is presumed to have been written by a Londoner named Richard Johnson (1573–1659), whose initials appear at the end of a forty-page booklet entitled *The History of Tom Thumbe, the Little, for his small stature surnamed, King Arthvrs Dwarfe: Whose Life and adventures contain many strange and wonderful accidents, published for the delight of merry Time-spenders.* Today the only known copy is in the Pierpont Morgan Library in New York City, where the research for this version was done.

Tom Thumb was already a well-known name prior to Johnson's telling, however. William Fulke referred to Tom in 1579 in *Heskins Parleament Repealed*, as did Thomas Nashe in *Pierce Pennilesse* in 1592. Reginald Scot's *Discoverie of Witchcraft*, written in 1584, lists "Tom Thumbe" along with "spirits, witches, urchens, elves, hags, fairies, satyrs, pans, faunes, sylens, kit with the canstick, dwarfes, giants, imps" and many other characters used by servant maids that "so affrighted people in their childhood that we are afraid of our owne shadowes."

What is most interesting is that incidents in Tom's story closely parallel those of other famous stories that had not yet been recorded. For example, Tom has the benefit of a fairy godmother long before Cinderella. And like the later Jack the Giant Killer, Tom meets a giant who threatens to ". . . grind his bones"; indeed, Tom's and Jack's tales have so many similarities that it is conceivable that they sprang from the same source. The character of Tom also has many popular counterparts around the world, such as *le petit poucet* in France and *Inchling* in Japan, to mention but two.

To be sure, Tom's name has been used more frequently in nursery literature than that of any other hero, for he is proof that—no matter what one's disadvantages—nothing can conquer the true spirit of courage and adventure.

The costumes and environments depicted in the illustrations of this book are loosely based on those of twelfth-century England, and the borders and ornamentation are inspired by manuscripts of the same era. The simple stylings of that period seem fitting for this lighthearted and timeless tale; and who knows—Tom Thumb's fantastic adventures may have sprung from stories told long before the sixteenth century.